First published in Great Britain 1999
by Orion Children's Books
a division of the Orion Publishing Group Ltd
Orion House
5 Upper St Martin's Lane
London WC2H 9EA

Copyright © 1999 Selina Young

Designed by Louise Millar

The right of Selina Young to be identified as
author and illustrator of this work has been asserted.

Printed in Italy

My Favourite Word Book

chocolate, dinosaur, sea, socks

words and pictures
by Selina Young

Orion
Children's Books

Pat the cat

Patch the dog

Smudge the rabbit

Ladybird that was just passing.

fire station

shops

airport

cinema

building site

park

pavement

Town

road

hospital

school

factory

garage

train

train station

library

dentist

litter bin

surgery

hotel

roundabout

street lamp

7

Travel

balloon

bus

motorbike

aeroplane

bike

ship

I can't find Patch and Smudge, can you?

submarine

8

9

playhouse

bricks

chairs

table

painting

sand

blackboard

chalk

dressing up box

friends

teacher

School

Welcome to our school olivia

Kermit

How many paintings can you count?

I ♥ Reading

fat cat's hat

stories

Ned

Red fox

Max

monkey's

fairy tales

crayons

paint

books

toilets

globe

scissors

apron

numbers

The little red hen went cluck, cluck, cluck!

boy

girl

lunch box

letters

tape recorder

pegs

clock

computer

pencils

glue

paper

water

coats 11

hair

eyebrows

eyes

teeth

ear

mouth

neck

chin

shoulders

heel

hand

nails

thumb

knee

leg

ankle

nose

face

tummy

13

doctor

Jobs

what day is it today?

teacher

nurse

ballet dancer

computer operator

farmer

actor

hairdresser

dentist

photographer

footballer

lorry driver

14

fireman

fisherman

builder

mechanic

acrobat

clown

shopkeeper

singer

chef

astronaut

what will you be Toby?

15

Car

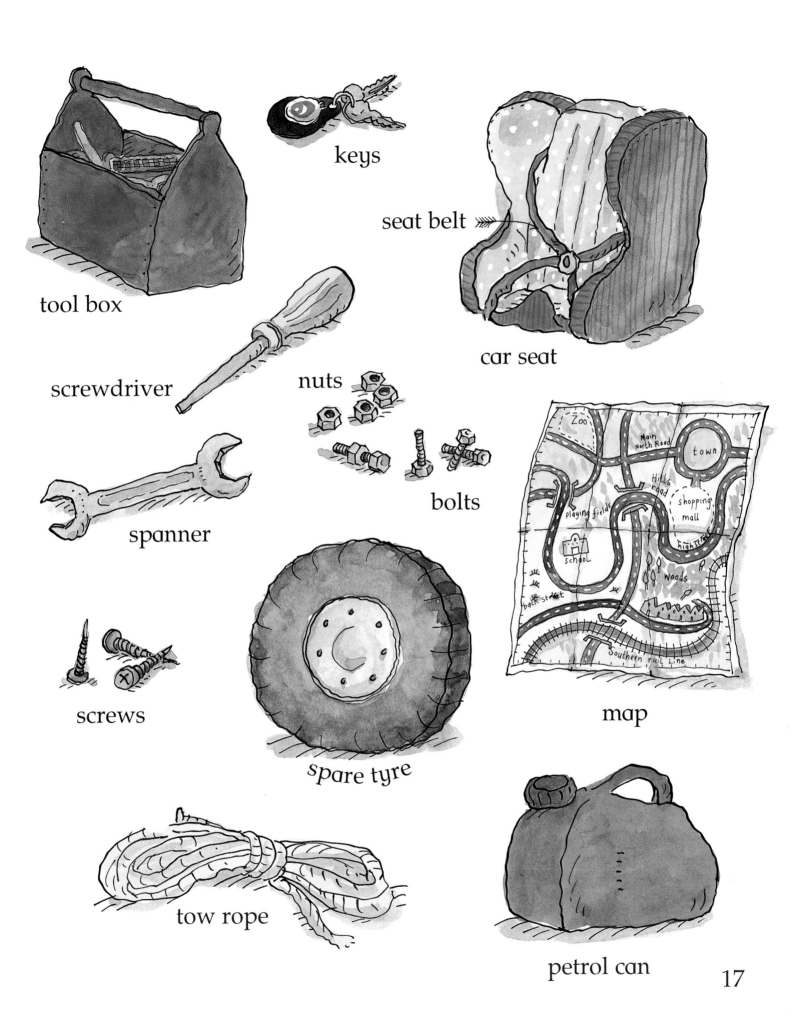

tool box

keys

seat belt

car seat

screwdriver

nuts

spanner

bolts

screws

spare tyre

map

tow rope

petrol can

17

House

roof

light

floor

attic

mirror

shower

taps

bath

basin

dressing table

bed

bathroom

bedroom

wall

settee

cushions

bookcase

This is my kennel

Patch

table

fire

TV

lounge

stairs

19

Housework

polish

duster

vacuum cleaner

brush

dustpan

Farm

farmer

hello

eggs

hen house

hen

cockadoodledooo

chicks

cockerel

kennel

sheepdog

quack

duck

ducklings

pond

calf   cow

bull   barn

How many sheep can you count?

pig

pigsty

piglet

22

Machines

breakdown lorry

forklift

steam roller

crane

concrete mixer

road drill

car transporter

petrol tanker

digger

dumper truck

bulldozer

jelly

sandwiches

sausages-on-sticks

Birthday

Happy Birthday to you

popcorn

balloons

streamers

camera

friends

How many chocolate fingers are left?

26

presents

birthday cards

crisps

wrapping paper

cake

candles

plate

straw

cups

party hat

cakes

chocolate fingers

spoon

27

face paints

necklace

beads

thread

dice

board game

teaset

doll's house

puzzle

finger puppets

horse

sit up dolly

comb

buggy

Department Store

tea
coffee
juice
biscuits
buns
trays

café

puzzles
bricks
dolls
car
ball
soft toys
newspapers

toys

books
freezer
microwave
TV
video
computer
stereo
washing machine
vacuum cleaner
fridge
dishwasher

31

Clothes

socks

sun hat

vest

pants

scarf

tights

shirt

hairband

T-shirt

skirt

trousers

swimsuit

dress

when it's hot I like wearing my swimsuit

trainers

coat

shoes

sweatshirt

woolly hat

cap

gloves

belt

jumper

dressing gown

nightie

pyjamas

when it's cold we wrap up warm

shorts

leotard

cardigan

ribbon

patch

boots

33

Cake

Mum

apron

bowl

Yummy!
I like
baking.

oven

scales

wooden
spoon

baking tin

mixer

recipe

flour

sieve

oven gloves

eggs

sugar

salt

chocolate
buttons

butter

whisk

jug

timer

icing

crumbs

knife

plate

cake

35

Play

roundabout

children

sandpit

book

basketball

football

tennis

roller blades

music

hopscotch

CHALK

36

climbing frame

swings

playtent

slide

see-saw

skateboard

bike

cards

I'm playing hide-and-seek with Patch and Pat, can you help me find them?

37

deckchair

sunhat

suncream

picnic

shells

windsurfer

38

sandcastle

sand

sea

waves

starfish

beach

Seaside

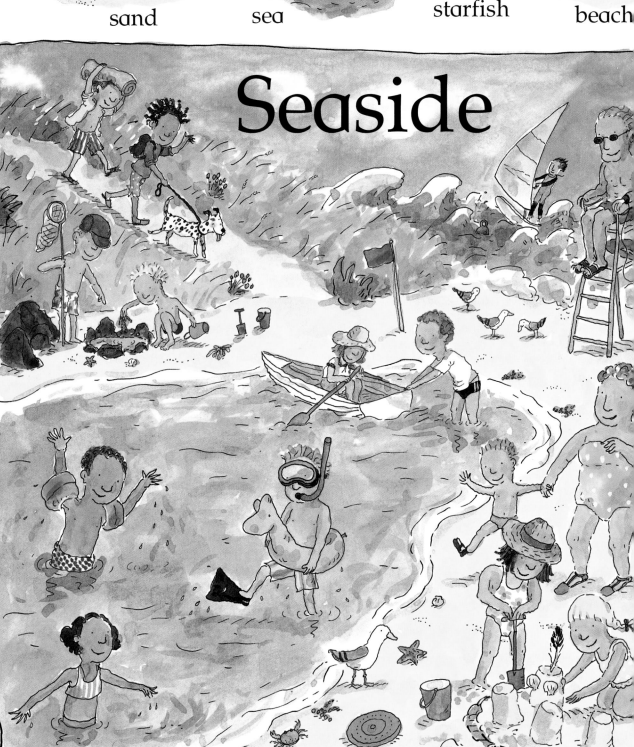

towel

flag

boat

cliffs

crab

buoy

seaweed

rock pool

spade

bucket

swimsuit

trunks

umbrella

sunglasses

How many seagulls can you count?

life guard

kite

seagull

armbands

people

39

Animals

chimpanzee

snake

giraffe

tiger

I live in India

lion

crocodile

zebra

I'm strong

elephant

parrot

rhinoceros

40

leopard

kangaroo

I can run fast

I like Jumping

bear

I'm good at swimming

hippopotamus

wolf

panda

antelope

camel

penguin

gorilla

I like the Snow

polar bear

ostrich

41

jars

Supermarket

fizzy drink

biscuits

COOKIES
COOKIES
COOKIES

jam

bottles

pasta

flour

FLOUR
FLOUR
FLOUR

tea

coffee

Pure Orange

grape

sugar

FRUIT and VEGETABLES

juice

bananas

cucumbers

onions

oranges

apples

lettuces

carrots

crisps

lemons

potatoes

tomatoes

42

43

Food

milk

bread

yoghurt

cheese

apple

orange

chocolate

spaghetti

pasta shapes

toast

butter

jam

baked beans

burger

sausages

fish fingers

grapes

ice cream

ice lolly

strawberries

sweets

chips

ketchup

crisps

raisins

biscuits

orange squash

pancakes

syrup

salt and pepper

eggs

pizza

hot chocolate

I love pizzas, do you?

honey

cake

sweetcorn

45

Painting

paper

crayon

handprints

tissue paper

picture

paints

water jar

felt pens

glue

glitter

apron

scissors

string

paintbrushes

47

Dinosaurs

Iguanodon

Triceratops

teeth

claws

body

Please do not touch

tail

baby

48

Tyrannosaurus Rex

flower pots

snail

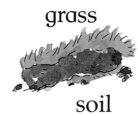
grass

soil

worm

butterfly

weeds

bird

fork

tree

petals

daisy

Garden

watering can

sunflower

bee

pond

frog

50

rake

fence

branches

leaves

gate

flowers

flower bed

nest

hedge

peas

shed

How many flower pots can you count?

Do you like playing in the garden?

vegetable patch

tomatoes

lettuce

caterpillar

51

Pets

gerbil

guinea pig

mice

hamster

lizard

cat

dog

goldfish

52

canary

puppy

kitten

rabbit

tortoise

pony

mouse

53

Swimming pool

slide

lifeguard

rubber ring

goggles

swimming hat

float

Sea

land

sea

stingray

Can you count all the fish?

lifejacket

sail

jellyfish

boat

sailor

lighthouse

whale

dolphin

shark

octopus

anchor

swordfish

seahorse

coral

diver

eel

turtle

57

Music

orchestra

trumpet

triangle

hand bells

drum

violin

bow

recorder

tambourine

guitar

music

cymbals

piano

59

Theme park

ghost train

cave

dragon

fairy

fairy forest

king

knight

ENTRANCE

Howdy!

Hello

ticket

60 cowboy

alien

Book

I like the big bad wolf best!

page

book

Little Red Riding Hood takes a basket of goodies to her Granny in the woods. But is it Granny in Bed? What big teeth she has......

LITTLE RED RIDING HOOD

bookmark

Jack and the Beanstalk

Three Little Pigs

Snow White and the Seven Dwarfs

Cinderella

Little Red Riding Hood

stars

bat

woof

toothbrush

pyjamas
toothpaste

book

pillow

Cinderella

night light

duvet

curtain

LETTERS

smudge

64

Index

Here is the index to help you find all the words in this book.

Remember the page number next to the word you choose and then turn to that page.

First choose a word from the index.

Then look for your word. Let's find bones!

Did you see me on every page?

Dd

Ee

Ff

Gg

Sometimes I ask questions, sometimes I'm hiding.

goldfish 52
gorilla 41
Gran 21
Grandpa 61
grapes 44
grass 50
guinea pig 52
guitar 59

Hh

hair 13
hairband 32
hairdresser 14
hammer 28
hamster 52
hand 13
hand bells 59
handprints 46
hay 23
head 12
headlights 16
hedge 51
heel 13
helicopter 9
hen house 22
hen 22
hill 23
hippopotamus 41
honey 45
hopscotch 36
horse 23, 29
hose 21
hospital 6
hot chocolate 45
hot dogs 61
hotel 7
house 18
housework 20

Ii

ice 5
ice cream 44
ice lolly 44
icing 35
Iguanodon 48

Jj

Jack and the Beanstalk 63
jam 42, 44
jars 42
jelly 26
jellyfish 56
jewellery 31
jobs 14
jug 35
juice 30, 42
jumper 33
jumpers 31

Kk

kangaroo 41
kennel 22
ketchup 45
keys 17
king 60
kitchen 19
kite 39
kitten 53
knee 13
knife 35
knight 60

Ll

lady 31
lamb 23
land 56
lawnmower 21
leaves 51
leg 13
lemons 42
leopard 41
leotard 33
letters 11
lettuce 51
lettuces 42
library 7
lifeguard 39, 54
lifejacket 56
lift 31
light 18
lighthouse 56
lion 40
litter bin 7
Little Red Riding Hood 63
lizard 52
lockers 55
lorry driver 14
lounge 18
lunch box 11

Mm

machines 24
magician 61
man 31
map 17
material 21
meat 43
mechanic 15

Try to find me.

Whoops, now I'm late for tea!